Usborne Farmyard Tales
Sticker Stories

Tractor in Trouble

Heather Amery

Illustrated by Stephen Cartwright

Language consultant: Betty Root
Series editor: Jenny Tyler

How to use this book

This book tells a story about the Boot family. They live on Apple Tree Farm.
Some words in the story have been replaced by pictures.
Find the stickers that match these pictures and stick them over the top.
Each sticker has the word with it to help you read the story.

Some of the big pictures have pieces missing.
Find the stickers with the missing pieces to finish the pictures.

A yellow duck is hidden in every picture. When you have found the duck you can put a sticker on the page.

This is Apple Tree Farm.

Mrs. Boot, the farmer, has two

called Poppy and Sam. She also has a

called Rusty.

Ted works on the farm.

He helps Mrs. Boot. Ted looks after the

and all the other machines.

He always wears an old brown  .

Today it is very windy.

There is lots of snow on the ground. The wind is blowing the  and it is very cold. Poppy and Sam play in the  .

Ted waves to Poppy and Sam.

"Where are you going, Ted?" they shout.

"I'm going to the field to see if the 

are all right," says  .

Ted stops the tractor by the gate.

 goes into the sheep field. He climbs up

a  and nails down the roof of the

sheep shed to make it safe.

Poppy and Sam hear a terrible crash.

“What’s that?” says  . “I don’t know.

Let’s go and look,” says Poppy. They run

down the field.  goes too.

The wind has blown a tree down!

"The tree's fallen on top of the tractor,"

shouts  . "Come on. We must

help Ted," says  .

children
tractor
I found the duck!
Ted
I found the duck!
tree
I found the duck!
ladder
I found the duck!
branches
I found the duck!
Dolly
tractor
Sam
hat
I found the duck!
Ted
Rusty
sheep
house
apple
I found the duck!
tractor

I found the duck!
tree
Poppy
I found the duck!
Ted
dog
I found the duck!
hat
I found the duck!
I found the duck!
tractor
Sam
I found the duck!
barn
I found the duck!
branches
tree
I found the duck!
horse
I found the duck!
ropes
Ted

“What are you going to do, Ted?”

Poor Ted is very upset. The  has scratched the . He can’t even get into the cab.

“Run to the house and find your mother.”

“Ask her to fetch Farmer Dray,” says  .

“He might be able to help.” Poppy and Sam

run back to the  as fast as they can.

Soon Farmer Dray comes.

He is wearing a hard  . He brings his

 . Her name is Dolly. She is big and

gentle. Dolly is strong enough to help Ted.

Farmer Dray starts up his chain saw.

“I’ll cut up the first,” he says.

He cuts off the branches that have fallen

on the  .

Dolly starts work.

Farmer Dray ties two thick

to Dolly's harness. He ties the other ends to the

big  on the ground.

Dolly pulls and pulls.

She works very hard until all the  are pulled away. "Well done, Dolly," says Farmer Dray and he gives her an .

Ted climbs into the tractor.

He waves to  and Farmer Dray.

"Thank you very much," says .

They all go back to the farmyard.

Ted finds some paint and a brush.

He paints over the scratches. "The

will soon look as good as new," he says.

Cover design and digital manipulation by Nelupa Hussain
This edition first published in 2005 by Usborne Publishing Ltd, Usborne House, 83-85 Saffron Hill, London EC1N 8RT, England. www.usborne.com
 First published in America 2005. U.E. Printed in Malaysia.